Dinosaur Disaster!

Illustrated by Sarah Jennings

Picture Corgi

Read more books in this series:

My Moving Day

The Friendship Bench

Show and Tell

DINOSAUR DISASTER!
A PICTURE CORGI BOOK 978 0 552 57239 2
Published in Great Britain exclusively for Sainsbury's
by Picture Corgi, an imprint of Random House Children's Publishers UK
A Random House Group Company
This edition published 2014

1 3 5 7 9 10 8 6 4 2

Copyright © Random House Children's Publishers UK, 2014
Illustrated by Sarah Jennings
The right of Sarah Jennings to be identified as the illustrator of this work has
been asserted in accordance with the Copyright, Designs and Patents Act 1988.
Picture Corgi Books are published by Random House Children's Publishers UK,
61–63 Uxbridge Road, London W5 5SA
www.randomhousechildrens.co.uk
www.randomhouse.co.uk
Addresses for companies within The Random House Group Limited can be found at:
www.randomhouse.co.uk/offices.htm
THE RANDOM HOUSE GROUP Limited Reg. No. 954009
A CIP catalogue record for this book is available from the British Library.
Printed in China

MIX
Paper from
responsible sources
FSC® C020056

The Random House Group Limited supports the Forest Stewardship Council® (FSC®), the leading international
forest-certification organisation. Our books carrying the FSC label are printed on FSC®-certified paper.
FSC is the only forest-certification scheme supported by the leading environmental organisations, including
Greenpeace. Our paper procurement policy can be found at www.randomhouse.co.uk/environment

Hello, I'm Molly and this is my friend Max.
And we LOVE dinosaurs!
We have dinosaur posters, dinosaur games and dinosaur pyjamas.
I even have a dinosaur cat called Whiskers. (He is not really a dinosaur.)

Last night we had a dinosaur sleepover in our dino den.
And today, for a special treat, Dad is taking me and Max
to the dinosaur exhibition at the museum. He even promised
to buy me my own T-Rex toy from the museum shop!

Max and I are so excited that we actually become dinosaurs.

We are great big hungry diplodocuses eating yummy dinopops.
(Diplodocuses are a bit messy!)
We are stomping stegosauruses going up the stairs.

We are charging triceratops chasing down the hall.

And then Dad says we need to please stop being dinosaurs
– it's time to get ready.

But we are still dinosaurs when we set off for the museum.
We are soaring pteranodons when we zoom along the street.

We are roaring tyrannosauruses when we're sitting on the bus.
Dad says if we can't behave properly then we won't go to see the
dinosaurs at all.

At least we haven't eaten any of the passengers (and some of them
look quite tasty!).

We have to be very careful at the museum because it is full of precious things like bones and models. Dad says the dinosaurs might be a bit scary – but that's just silly. There won't be any real dinosaurs, because all the dinosaurs died a really long time ago.

Anyway, we are big brave dinosaurs and we are not scared of anything!

Max has a not-very-brave moment – and so do I!

But we both feel better when Dad explains that this is a special robot
dinosaur and that it's friendly.

Soon we are feeling ready to explore. There are lots of signs saying
DO NOT TOUCH and lines saying DO NOT CROSS, so we are careful.

The Coelophysis
really liked to
eat meat!

The
Parasaurolophus
ate tree leaves
and pine needles.

DO
NOT
CROSS

Miniature
Model

Coelophysis skeleton

Velociraptor

Fossil dragonfly
from Jurassic times

DO NOT
TOUCH

DO NOT
TOUCH

Dinosaur
egg fossils

We find a huge dinosaur skeleton.
"Do dinosaurs have ghosts?" asks Max. "Woooooooooooo!"
I look at its ginormous dinosaur teeth. "Imagine how big the dinosaur's toothbrush would have to be!"

Tyrannosaurus Rex skeleton

DO NOT CROSS

Before long we are big
brave dinosaurs again.
We are roaring and soaring . . .

We are stomping up the stairs . . .
and we are charging down the corridors.

The people who know everything
about dinosaurs look a bit cross.

We learn that there are over seven hundred different kinds of dinosaur. Some dinosaurs were as small as chickens, and some were as heavy as seventeen elephants, or as long as five buses!

Diplodocus

Stegosaurus skele

Dinosaur footprint

DO NOT TOUCH

· Dilophosaurus ·

Some dinosaurs were very slow and mainly just sat around munching. But we like being the fast kind of dinosaur, the kind that run and run and run . . .

Pterodactyl

Dinosaur eggs

Dinosaur nest

DO NOT TOUCH

Bactrosaurus

Compso

And then something bad happens . . .

Pterodactyl

Spinosaurus

Stegosaurus

Ankylosaurus

DO NOT TOUCH

Bactrosaurus

DO NOT TOUCH

Compsognathus

We set off a very loud alarm by accident.

DO
NOT
CROSS

Velociraptor skeleton

And Dad turns into the scariest dinosaur of all . . .

Dad shouts that we can never come to the museum again.
I will not get a toy T-Rex. And worst of all, we have to go and
say sorry to the people who know everything about dinosaurs.
(Dinosaurs do not like saying sorry to people they don't know –
especially when the people look cross.)

We find the biggest person who knows everything about
dinosaurs and say we're sorry.
We tell him that we were trying to be like all the dinosaurs,
and how much we like them, and . . .

. . . the person who knows everything about dinosaurs (who is also called Mr Smith) is NICE!

The Stegosaurus had a brain the size of a tangerine.

Stegosaurus

He stops being cross and tells us about some of the dinosaurs
that were a bit more quiet.

Triceratops
needed big
horns to protect
themselves
from the T-Rex!

DO NOT
CROSS

Triceratops

Dinosaur
footprint

At lunch Max and I are the quietest dinosaurs we can be.

Dad says that he is sorry for shouting, and that we were very good for saying sorry.

Then, on the way home Dad does something amazing!
He gives us two T-Rex toys – one each. We are very excited
and happy – but we play very quietly . . . we don't want Dad to
become a dinosaur again!

Max and I probably know more about dinosaurs than anybody in our whole school now. Mum says we could definitely become famous dinosaur discoverers.

I'd like to discover a new superdinosaur.
But I don't think Whiskers would be very pleased!